Mermaid & Her Vampires

By David Evans

Table of Contents:

Chapter 1: Genesis

Luscius gushed, "I can't believe you two fought again."

Iris and Rose glared at each other angrily before turning to face Luscius who was standing directly in front of them.

Iris said in a sweet voice, "Come now Luscius, It's not my fault." Rose retorted angrily, "No She started it, Luscius.

"What am I going to do with both of you? you told me that you would change.

“Do you want me to inform Miss Catherine about the two of you?" Luscius enquired.

"No!" The females all spoke at once.
Luscius groaned.

"You most definitely don't have to do that, Damon dear." Iris said.

"Yes, yes, we'll be on our best behavior. Promise." Rose agreed.

Rose and Iris briefly glanced at each other to glare at themselves, then went back to looking at Damon with pleading eyes.

"Not that I really give a damn, but why the hell started it anyway? Because they would do well to first apologise" He queried.

Iris and Rose made opposite-side gestures with their middle fingers.

"Heyyy!" Iris began to quake when Luscius spoke in a loud voice.

Rose swiftly retorted, "Don't believe her because she's your sister.

Iris swiftly added, "Don't believe her because she's your assistant.

"I have nothing to say to any of you. You never stop unnecessarily getting on my nerves."

"You know what, just have a seat; I'm exhausted! But if it happens again, I won't hesitate to report you both to Miss Catherine. Got it?" Luscius continued.

Iris and Rose nodded while lowering their gazes.

Luscius said, "Now go. Just go...Aiish," and turned to face his desk again. Books were scattered on it.

Iris and Rose exchanged angry looks, before hissing and growling.

Luscius replied, "I can hear that.

Rose walked away while Iris laughed.

Iris chuckled and said, "You can hear that because your part vampire, genius. He and she were now close.

Looking at his books, Luscius remarked, "It's called being a hybrid, naughty."

She hissed, "Anyone! “Step up to your seat. I'm here trying to study, "Luscius spoke while keeping his gaze fixed on the book.

"Do you never grow or change?”

“What's the point of studying when you can pass with your abilities?"

"You can hear him. You know, he's a vampire, "said Luscius

"Dummy, he can't hear me. Vampires are unable to hear faint whispers from other vampires. They’re only able to hear from puny humans. You just caught Rose hissing; you missed my snarl."

Luscius shook his head, "Whatever.

Iris grinned and turned around once again.

"Why must he be so attractive?”

“He’s quite attractive. Oh, dear heart"

"Why not tell him instead of telling me?” "Luscius enquired.

Unexpectedly, a student entered the classroom. After scanning the area, he walked to Luscius "The staff room is where Miss Catherine needs you right now. In addition, the teaching assistant "He spoke.

"Why? Is there a problem?" After asking, Luscius put his book down.

He said, "I don't know," and walked away. After getting up, Luscius went to Rose.

Miss Catherine wants us, hey.

"What? Why? Did anyone inform her about the altercation between Iris and I?"

Luscius replied, "I don't know, but I suppose we will have to go and see for ourselves.

Rose took a deep breath and stood. Later, they both left together. Iris though, continued to fix her gaze on Zeke, now he was dozing off.

Before passing out on his desk, he was listening to music. Luscius approached him and sat down next to him, admiring his attractive features.

"How is it possible to sleep so attractively?" Luscius enquired.

Lily and Mera, two of Iris's pals, arrived to meet her there.

Iris? Called Lily.

Iris silenced her with "Ssh."

"Gosh, you might wake him up," said Iris. Anna shook her head and said, "I wonder why you’re head over heels with an unserious vampire.

Iris remarked, "Not your business, witch

"I appreciate the compliment. I mean, I’m a witch.

Sorceress is the appropriate term at this point, got it? I practice sorcery. Anna grinned.

Iris rolled her eyes, "Whatever."

As Iris continued to observe him, he suddenly opened his eyes. She exhaled and got to her feet, Zeke cocked his head up and flashed a flash of red in his eyes.

""What's that scent?" "Do you smell it?" Coolly, he enquired.

Even the sound of his voice makes me like him, Iris reasoned.

"Well? Do you smell that?" He sniffed and asked again. His eyes once more flashed red.

"What? I'm powerless, you have the finest nose ever. Thus, you can smell anything, she winked. "Your vampire nose is so animated.

Zeke abruptly got to his feet and left without saying anything. Why would I prefer Zeke when there's Luscius? As she grinned.

Hello, witch. You think Iris will approve of her half-brother? Lily enquired.

Let her go. In either case, she’ll be spewing trash, I'm sure. What did Zeke smell anyway, causing him to leave in that manner? Aiish! Such a pain! said Iris.

Chapter 2: Gathering

In the Staff Room, Melissa and Lola Lake are our newest students and your classmates, respectively. Said Miss Catherine.

"Greetings to you both. I'm Lena Dora, the student helper."

Melissa and Lola joined together to say, "Thank you and a pleasure to meet you too.

“Luscius introduced himself as "Luscius Red, the class president." John shook his hand as Melissa grinned and nodded.

"You ought to accompany them to class, I'll be right behind you, "said Miss Catherine.

Luscius said, "Join me.

Melissa instantly grabbed his hand as he started to walk. He hastily removed his hand as he turned to face her.

“Why is it?” He kindly questioned.

Please, Melissa pleaded, "I can't walk."

Luscius studied her legs with his eyes. Except for Lola, everyone was giving them perplexed looks.

"Your legs look great," he remarked.

"No!" Melissa's cry caused Luscius and the others to start shaking.

"I've reached my breaking point, please provide a hand. It might come off if I move just a little bit, "said Melissa.

"Pardon me?" Luscius enquired.

Lola chuckled, "She wants to use the restroom."

"Please take me." Melissa folded her legs together and begged.

“What are you waiting for, Luscius?” The scowl of Miss Catherine.

Luscius turned to face Lola

"Are you really her family?” Can't you manage it?”

“Why not transport her?" He queried.

"I’m unable to sprint while carrying her, I might trip, "said Lola

Melissa cried out, "Oh no, please...help, class president," rubbing her hands together.

"Luscius!" Loudly, Miss Catherine said.

"I absolutely detest this, shit. Cling on "Luscius Spoke as he knelt down.

Get inside, he murmured.

Melissa replied, "Thank you," and leapt up onto his back. Luscius carried her hard while grunting.

He exited the staff room hastily.

While Rose chewed her lower lip, John grinned. Lady Catherine chuckled.

"I can't believe she did this on her first day at school" Miss Catherine laughed. Other teachers joined her.

"Cute kids" Miss Catherine inhaled deeply.

"Who's she now?" Rose thought, feeling jealous

Zeke hurried inside the staff area; the fragrance was emanating from there. the aroma of an unidentified sweet blood.

He had never, before in his whole vampire existence encountered the wonderful aroma of such blood.

"Huh? Zeke? Why are you in this place? When she noticed him, Miss Catherine questioned in shock.

Zeke scanned the area, it's gone. I can smell it out there now," he thought, turning away without pausing to look back.

What's his issue? said Miss Catherine. "Drop down. Here we are "While panting, Luscius said.

Melissa vigorously shook his head while holding him at the back.

“What is it once more?” He asked groggily.

"It might flow if I descend. Please let me inside "Melissa beseeched.

"Geez! What a waste of a first day! Just murder me! You expect me to enter a women's restroom in what manner?" He inquired.

Melissa instantly put her hands over his eyes to close them.

"You won't see anything, so don't worry. Please move quickly so I don't urinate on your body."

"F*ck! No!" Luscius spoke before quickly entering.

There were girls there who screamed, he was getting hit by some. Luscius continued repeating he was sorry and that he hadn't seen anything.

"Drop down. Here we are "While panting, Luscius said.

Iris, who was washing her hand in the sink, was surprised and shocked when her gaze fell on him.

"What's he doing here? Who's that Iris paused and sniffed. Her eyes turned light blue.

"What's this sweet smell?" Iris muttered, allowing her fangs to develop.

She wanted to bite and drink the blood, it was coming from the girl behind Luscius, obviously.

As she wanted to grab onto Melissa with her long sharp fingers which were now growing, someone held her from behind.

She turned behind and saw Zeke. looking at her with his red-looking eyes. His fangs were not yet out.

"Zeke What are you?”

"Leave" He commanded.

"Now" He commanded again.

Iris sighed, returning to normal with her eyes, teeth, and even her fingers. She made a deliberate exit.

The girls who noticed him yelled.

"Why are the attractive men now entering the women's restroom?"

"What's going on with the men's room right now?" "Zeke altered his eyeglasses. Nice."

Zeke remained silent. The females hastened out as he simply strolled past them. He locked the door when they had gone.

Within one of the restrooms. When Melissa was brought down, she hurriedly removed her skirt. Luscius quickly averted his gaze. He hurriedly walked out after turning around.

"What's wrong with you!" He exclaimed.

"I'm sorry," she said.

Luscius was suddenly pushed out through the door and Zeke made his way in.

He was looking at Melissa now, she was about to urinate. Her skirt was down, she is only wearing her tights.

"Sweet blood" He smiled and smacked his lips.

Luscius, who was still outside, shook his head.

"Who was that?" Could that be a girl?" He thought.

"Ah!" He suddenly heard Melissa scream.

Luscius quickly opened the door, Zeke was now about to bite her with his long fangs. His eyes were now deep red.

His hand flew out, he was this close to biting her when Luscius quickly held his mouth and Zeke ended up biting Luscius's palm instead which hurt him a little bit because he was a half vampire hybrid.

"Eww!" Zeke exclaimed and slapped Luscius's hand away.

Melissa looked at them, her eyes saw little blood on Zeke's attractive lips. She also saw blood and teeth marks on Luscius's fair palm.

Melissa felt her urine leaving her, the two watched her in shock.

Afterwards, she passed out.

Zeke and Luscius quickly took their hands to carry her. but they couldn't, the smell was now different. Smell of urine.

They ended up walking out.

"Geez, that was- Zeke inhaled deeply.

Luscius glared at him. “You’re an asshole" He muttered. Zeke smirked at him and wiped the blood off his lip.

They both turned to the door after hearing a knock. Zeke opened it and Lola barged in.

Chapter 3: Class

★ ★ ★ ★

A Half-Hour Before Lissa's Arrival

"Lissa? Lola?" You two done? Hurry?" You both and I are running late "Their 25-year-old older sister Lorna acknowledged as much.

She was waiting for her two younger sisters, both of whom were 18 years old, outside by her car.

She saw them hurry out of the home and smiled. Her grin vanished and was replaced by a startled look.

"Lissa?" "What's that?" Lorna enquired, Lola grinned.

"What are you going to use three enormous water bottles for?" Lorna enquired.

Since the previous night her birthday" she has been complaining of excruciating and unquenchable thirst," Lola said.

Lorna gave Melissa a glance.

"Is it real? "

Melissa chuckled.

"Why?" "Do you think it's the symptoms of turning into a vampire? You don't have to worry... I was never bitten"

"Let me see your gills" Lorna said. Melissa brought down the collar of her shirt and removed the glamor she placed on the sides of her neck to expose three open slashes, gill filaments, on her neck.

Unbeknownst to everyone, she and her sisters, her family, were all some of the rarest of creatures in the world; they were mermaids.

Yes, mermaids were real and they very much exist, just like vampires. They just aren't that many of them.

An endangered species, some might say they were. They would be right. Lora raised her right hand to place her fingers into one of those filaments to get a feel for her inner rakers. Melissa's face began to twitch a little from her sister's touch, they were ticklish. She let out a small giggle as Lorna brought out her hand from her neck's side.

"There's not nearly as much moisture as I would have expected." Lorna said as she rubbed her index finger to her thumb, testing how slippery they were.

"You aren't swimming enough; didn't you take a dive in the pool yesterday? Today?"

"Aaah... I did... "

Lorna raised a brow. "Lissa, you know as a mermaid you need water far more than what the average human being does.

Water is life, we can't survive without it. You know all this." "I know, I know. I'm sorry. But I am taking my swims. Just not for that long, I guess."

"Why's that?" Asked Lorna. She stayed silent. Lorna frowned, then raising both brows, asked "Boy trouble?"

"What the depths made you think that! Of course not!"

"Whatever. Just be careful okay. I might not be around if you get in trouble you know. You have to take care of yourself. Promise?" "I promise."

Lorna sighed and nodded. She was a new member of Grim Hunters, meaning she was going to hunt down supernatural beings and make them go imprisoned and vampires were sure part of them.

They had moved to the city, from their home in the sea after Lorna got a job to be a Grim Hunter.

"Come on, girls. Were late" Lorna said and entered the car.

Lola giggled, and ran to the front seat, where she sat with her sister while Melissa sat at the back alone.

As soon as her butt touched the seat, she opened one of the bottles, and sat the opening into her mouth, drinking the water like her life depended on it.

Lorna looked back and watched as Melissa drank the water. She arched her brows, trying to wonder what was going on with Melissa.

"Melissa?" Lorna called.

Melissa inhaled deeply and stopped drinking.

She covered the bottle, with the water, remaining past quarter.

"Noona!" Lola called, before Lorna would say anything.

Lorna took her eyes off Melissa and took them to Lola.

"What's it, Lola?" she asked.

"Look at the whole water she drank! Wow" Lola gushed.

Lorna forced a smile. "I can see that, Lola."

Lorna took her eyes back to Melissa.

"Just so you remember, Melissa. There’s no restroom close by till we are at your school so just stay without drinking for a while"

Melissa breathed hard. "But I just can't hold it. I keep getting thirsty"

Lorna exhaled deeply and started the ignition. She began driving on the smooth road, down to her sister's new school by name, Ocean's High.

"Since when did you start having this kind of thirst?" Lorna asked.

"Just like how Lola mentioned. Since yesterday, immediately I clocked 18"

"You know what, don't get too worried. I'm going to check what's going on with you and get back to you later, got that?"

"Thank you, Noona " Melissa smiled.

"Here we go again" Melissa added and sighed heavily before taking back the opened bottle into her mouth and drinking away the last content.

She kept the bottle in the trash which was in the car and kept her head on the car rest. She looked up and sighed deeply.

Her hand touched the old pendant around her neck. She opened it and saw a picture of her real mum.

Though, her mother's face seemed to have been scratched away by a sharp object causing the pendant to be scratched white.

Though they were all mermaids, Melissa wasn't the biological sister of Lorna and Lola. Though, she was loved and cared for by both of them.

She really didn't know much about her life. She doesn't even know her mother's face but still, she has this love for her.

Lorna's mom found her and brought her home, and that was it.

Of course, Mrs Lake took her to be her daughter and raised her well with love and care before she

died one night in the woods, and that's because of a vampire.

That was the main reason, Lorna grew her hatred for vampires. She began to train hard to be a Grim Hunter so that she would revenge. Her mother's wrongful death and bring down the vampires living within and out from them.

On the pendant, exactly on the scratched face of her mum, she saw Date of birth was 11/09/2004.

That was her date of birth. She guessed her unknown mother whom she still had feelings for, was trying to pass her the message of when she was born.

Lola was also born in the same month and year with Lissa, which happened to be an exciting coincidence. Hers was however 04/09/2004.

Melissa began to feel pressed suddenly and up till now, she still craves water.

"What's happening to me?" She thought, getting worried already.

"Melissa?" Lola called.

"Yes?" Melissa Answered.

Lola looked back at her and smiled.

"I don't have a pen. I was wondering if you had another to spare, ``she said.

Melissa ran her eyes around, trying to remember.

"Sure, I do have two"

"Yes! Can I have one?" Lola gushed.

"Wait, let me get it, okay?"

Lola nodded and turned back to the front. Melissa closed the pendant necklace and quickly opened the next water bottle.

She couldn't hold the thirst anymore. She drank half of the content, inhaled deeply, and closed the bottle.

"That feels better," Melissa said, relieved.

She wiped the water off her mouth and took her bag pack which was sitting with her earlier.

She placed it on thigh and opened it. She made her hand find its way into her bag, trying to find the pen when something in there suddenly pierced her palm. “Oww," Melissa moaned.

"You, okay?" Lorna who heard the painful moan asked, worriedly while Lola quickly turned her head over.

"I'm fine" Melissa forced a smile.

Lola nodded and looked at the front away. Melissa sighed and got the pen out. The pen which was sharp with its cover missing seemed to have pierced her palm.

She closed her backpack zipper and looked at her palm which had a small cut. She was bleeding a bit.

Her eyes widened when she saw the cut closing right before her eyes. Her heart jumped and she blinked trying to see if it was real.

Her cut was already closed by now, she threw her hand down and swallowed hard.

"What was that?" She thought.

Lola turned over to her, she noticed the unusual look on Melissa's face.

"Melissa?" Lola called but her mind was already far away, so nobody knows.

"Melissa? Melissa?" Lola called, again.

"Yes?" She finally jerked to real life.

"What's wrong with you?" I've been calling you since" Lola said.

"I'm okay... I'm just a little pressed" Lola replied.

"See, I did warn you. I'm going to pull up here so that you can use the bushes but do hurry, I don't want anyone seeing you. I don't want complaints either, okay?" Lorna said.

Melissa nodded. “Lola? The pen" Lola reminded her.

"Oh, here" She gave her the pen which she collected, before muttering a thank you.

Melissa practised inhalation and exhalation before opening the car door, after Lorna had stopped the ignite.

Melissa walked down the woods and stopped in an enclosed area. She quickly pulled down her skirt, and even her underwear.

She bent down to avoid any eyes and began to ease herself away.

"This feels like it" She smiled, closing her eyes trying to feel the happiness of the load flowing away.

She stood up and wore her skirt back, and her underwear too. She opened her eyes and saw a handsome guy looking at her. Judging from his outfit, He seemed to be a student.

"Hey, sweet blood" He finally said in a whisper which sounded super sexy and cool.

She looked deeply at him and said nothing. Immediately his eyes sparked red, she screamed and ran away.

Zeke, who watched her, chuckled. "She smells so sweet"

"What's wrong?" Lorna asked, as she saw Melissa screaming, running towards the car. Lorna quickly started the ignition and rushed to her. Melissa opened the door, and she jumped in.

"Move! Move!" Melissa screamed.

Lorna got back to the road again. "What is it, Lissa?" Lorna asked.

"You're behaving like you saw a ghost or something" Lola said.

"I saw a. vamp...vampire!" Melissa panted.

"What?" "How do you know that?" Lola asked.

"Wait? You sure?!" Lorna asked.

"Yes! He referred to me as sweet blood and his eyes his eyes.

"You know what. Let's talk about it later at home. Come down now, we are here" Lorna said, and stopped the car.

Lola and Melissa walked out and looked at Lorna.

"Girls, so sorry but I must leave now. I should be at work, you know" Lorna said.

"Sure, bye, Noona" The duo said, and waved.

"Okay girls, bye. I've talked to your teacher already so just go to her in the staff room.

She will signal to you both" Lorna said and started the car.

She began reversing. "Girls!" Lorna suddenly screamed.

They both looked at her.

"Welcome to Ocean's High!" She screamed.

Lola and Melissa looked at each other and smiled before turning back to see the beautiful, huge school with a huge and all-around wall fence before their very eyes.

Chapter 4: Discussion

Lola snuck in. She first focused on Zeke before turning to Luscius. They were equally close to the restroom door. "Class president, where is my sister?" Lola queried.

Please call me Luscius, Luscius said.

"Good, then. Luscius what's going on? My sister? ... Melissa?" Lola queried.

Following a brief glance-exchange between Luscius and Jake, Doris turned to face them and shrugged.

Luscius said, pointing towards the door, "She's in here."

As Lola passed Zeke, he swiftly gave her a sniff. Lola undoubtedly took notice. She halted her steps and gave him a vicious glance.

"Did you just sniff me, you pervert?" She asked.

"Per what? Hey, young girl. mind what you say" Zeke uttered.

"Young girl?" Lola scoffed.

"As if we aren't both 18!" She yelled.

"Luscius, you tell her, tell her how old I am and let's watch her faint in surprise" Luscius chuckled, dramatically. Luscius eyed him.

"You fool, the only reason she's going to faint is because she might think you lied. So, get your act together."

Lola shook her head, watching them whisper and finally walked into the toilet where Melissa was.

"I smelt her, and her blood doesn't smell like sweet blood" Zeke told Luscius.

"Now, you're calling that innocent new girl, sweet blood. You almost killed her on her first day, I can't wait to hear her sister scream.

"Ah!" They both heard Lola's piercing cry, Luscius groaned and rubbed his brow with his palm as he said, "Said it."

Lola hurried outside and turned to face them. "What has become of her?" "Why doesn't she wake up?" Luscius, did you arrive late?"

"She has already peed herself, after all!" Zeke fixed his gaze on the door as Luscius let out a heavy sigh.

Melissa gently opened her eyes; she was already perishing from shame.

"Why would she urinate in front of two hot guys?"

"Zeke was the vampire she encountered in the woods, according to her second memories, which suddenly came to her."

"Is he here as a student?" Zeke grinned wryly.

"Oh no!" Out loud, she thought.

Melissa suddenly recalled when Zeke bit Jake's hand.

Wait, that person is a vampire and was intending to bite me! Melissa exhaled.

She hurriedly got out of the hospital bed, the school doctor was examining some paperwork on her desk across the room.

She was up when the doctor saw her and hurried to help.

Hey," how are you?" With a friendly smile, the female doctor enquired.

“Where am I?” Melissa inquired coolly. The door was getting knocked on, which the doctor and Lissa heard.

"Come in..." The doctor said

Zeke walked in with a smile on his face, his hands were pocketed.

"Oh, Jake. Why are you here?" The doctor asked.

"I came to see...her" Zeke replied, pointing at Melissa whose side was covered with a curtain.

"Do...you know her?" The doctor asked.

"No," Jake shook his head and kept his pointing finger back into his pocket.

"Then, why do you want to see her?"

"I have an unfinished business with her"

"Huh?" Okay then... but do make it quick.

"Sure thing" Jake said and pushed out the curtain. He finally entered and closed it back, he looked at Melissa whose eyes were closed.

"I know you ain't sleeping so open those eyes" he said.

Melissa didn't do or say anything.

Zeke inhaled deeply and placed his mouth close to her ear.

"You taste quite good, you know. So, open your eyes while I'm being nice"

Melissa gasped and raised her head up. As soon as she did that, her head collided hard with Zeke's nose, and he yelled in pain.

"Ah! Geez! How come your head hits hard like a brick!" He grunted, touching the tip of his nose.

"Oww" Melissa whimpered and touched her forehead.

"Aiish! My nose nearly broke due to you. He grumbled.

Melissa shuddered instantly when Melissa gazed at her.

She begged, "Please, please, don't kill me."

Zeke smiled and approached her from behind. “How could I?” You’re too sweet and delicious to murder right now.

He touched her face with his hand before holding her jaw. While keeping his grip on her jaw, he took her face into his. She returned his intense gaze as he continued to hold it.

“What do you want from me?” She asked.

"Your memories," he said with a menacing grin.

"How...I-

He moved his face closer to hers while still gripping her jaw, causing her to pause and forcefully swallow.

"Forget everything you saw. Forget about me too" He whispered to her.

He wasn't willing to risk it. “How would a new girl just know he was a vampire?” It was so fast!

His old human classmates weren't even aware so why would a mere girl like this, had to know about it on her first day of school.

Melissa felt her eyes swirling. She was beginning to feel dizzy. She shook her head and eventually she got back to reality.

Zeke opened his eyes in surprise. He wondered why the enchantment left her. “What was wrong?”

"What are you doing to me?" Melissa asked, weakly.

"Why didn't it work? She isn't supernatural, so why?" Zeke thought.

"Let go of me" Lola said and slapped his hand off her jaw. Jake stood upright and stared in space, in thoughts.

“Why am I not okay?” Why am I feeling so lightheaded? I'm feeling strange.

Her head dipped swiftly, but Zeke quickly grabbed hold of her face. She was placed back on the cushion as he grinned.

Finally, that worked, he said with a smile as he left.

He told the doctor to "wake" then left.

The doctor raised her head and gave it a shake.

"What happened just now?" She pondered. "Let's not talk about it. Your uniform is already dried so just change." Lola said and walked out.

"Hurry, our teacher is waiting for us in the class. We need to be introduced, ``she added, from outside.

As they made their way back to class, Lola joined arms with Melissa.

She remarked, "I can see you are better now, Melissa." Melissa gave her a glance. About, she questioned.

"At that point, you couldn't help but repeatedly sip water. I noticed it getting smaller.

"Oh, you're absolutely right. I also observed that I wasn't as thirsty as I had been this morning. I suppose I feel better now.

Melissa grinned and rested her head on Melissa's shoulders, saying, "That's a relief."

We have a lot of gorgeous males in our club, by the way. “Do you not believe we ought to have one each?” As soon as they arrived at the lobby, Lola questioned.

Some gossiped, slept, used phones, listened to music, and even used make ups.

“Count me out. But suit yourself” Melissa, said and unlinked her arm from Lola, since they were now sitting down.

Lola chuckled and looked around, before facing Melissa. Rose who was close to Melissa was somewhat busy since her eyes were on her opened books on the desk.

“So, who do you think would be preferable for me to date?” Lola whispered.

“Huh? Why are you asking me that?” Melissa questioned in surprise.

“I want you to pick a guy for me, a handsome one”

“Why should I?” It’s your heart and not mine” Melissa looked away.

“Aww…Come on, come on, Melissa, pretty please” Lola shook her whole body, talking cutely.

Melissa chuckled.

“Alright, let’s see, " she said and looked around. Her eyes fell on Luscius who was reading his book with an earpiece in his ear. He looked handsome with all possible concentration.

Melissa smiled inwardly and faced Lola

“Luscius is Mr. perfect” She winked

Lola chuckled while Rose stood up and banged her hand on her desk. She turned to the sisters and showed her hateful stare.

“If you both wanna keep being my seat mates, make sure not to gossip annoying utterances, got that?!” She shouted and hissed.

But we're not chatting up anyone, we are only discussing ourselves. Lola looked at her and said, "You didn't even hear us, so don't say anything rubbish.

“Doris. It's okay. Just Ignore," Melissa urged.

Zeke picked it up while his head was still on the desk and turned to look in the direction the noise was coming from.

Melissa and Lola, who was standing, were the first to get his attention. He turned his head just a little to the right as he recalled what Iris had said.

> "Why not read her thoughts again to discover what is going through it?"

He lowered his gaze and furrowed his brows. He was irritated when he finally had a chance to read her thoughts.

He swerved his head slightly to the right side and remembered what Iris said.

"Our assistant likes our class pres.?" He muttered.

"This is getting interesting," He added.

Chapter 5: Confab

After School

Iris and Luscius walked side to side as they all moved outside.

> "My babies…" Mrs Red, their mother gushed when she saw them.

> "Mum!" Iris yelped, and rushed into her mother's arms, hugging her tight.

Mrs Red reciprocated the hug before looking back at Luscius, she raised her brow.

“Won’t Luscius hug dear old mummy too?” She asked.

Luscius cleared his throat and looked around. He saw Melissa and Lola coming out, with their arms linked, amidst laughter and discussion. Luscius looked at Lissa and blinked his eyes away.

“Let’s just go, it's so embarrassing” He muttered and went into the car.

Iris scoffed and entered as well.

Mrs Red laughed and turned to Melissa. She smiled, looked away and entered the car. She started the ignition later.

“Who’s she?” Mrs Red asked.

“Who?” Luscius answered.

“The beautiful and sweet new girl whom I’ve never seen before. Her blood also smelt so good, never smelt such a unique and sweet blood before”

“…Mum?” Luscius shook his head, in annoyance.

“Oh goodness, Luscius. Sorry but it's the fact. You don’t have to worry; I gave up drinking blood long ago. Besides, I promised your father to behave humane.” Mrs Red winked.

“But mum, to be sincere, I’ve never smelt such blood. It is so sweet and tempting. Each time I stay with her, I feel like biting and drinking off her blood, but I just don’t wanna be exposed, neither do I want to die” Iris said.

"What? die?" Mrs Red laughed.

"Uhm… I guess. who knows, her blood might be toxic"

"Hmm… I think you are right. Anyways, this isn't what I wanted to discuss. I was even talking to Luscius then" Mrs Red said.

"So, as I was saying-" Mrs Red cleared her throat and briefly looked at Luscius at the back before turning back to the front.

"Do you like her?" Mrs Red asked.

"What!" Iris yelled and turned over to look at him.

Luscius glared hard.

“Why would I?” Mum, please…stop saying obnoxious and unsensible things”

“Sorry, geez, so… Does she like you?” Mrs Red asked.

“Why would I know?” It's her business” Luscius inhaled hard.

“Are you sure you weren’t born in the 1950s?” Iris mocked, shaking her head.

“What?” Luscius looked at her.

“Vampires these days are more active and powerful. We aren’t like those old mythological ones” Iris said.

“So?” Luscius eyed her.

“It's simple and short. What she is trying to say is that ``You can know if she likes you or not” Mrs Red said.

Luscius raised a brow, nonchalant. He really didn’t care.

“So, you expect me to read her mind? Don’t you think it's a privacy invasion? You know I’m clearly against that” Luscius said.

"Dummy, I'm more brilliant than you when it comes to paranormal studies"

"Kid yourself. There's nothing like that" Luscius scoffed.

"Wish there was. Just listen, whenever someone likes a vampire, the vampire won't be able to read the mind of the person anymore" Iris explained.

"Why?" Why's that?" Luscius asked.

"Don't really know, maybe it because the heart shut the mind reading powers in the vampire"

"So, for example, let's say, Rose

"Yuck!"

"Aiish! Okay, let's say, Melissa

"Sweet but yuck!"

"Aiish! Let's say Nora

"Hey, how dare my friend like you!"

"Darn it! It's just an example. Okay, let's use Anna"

"Forget it, she's taken"

"Pardon?" Luscius asked, confused.

“That little witch likes John but doesn’t wanna say it out”

“That doesn’t concern me. Okay, let's use… Renee. So, If Renee likes me, I won’t be able to read her mind?”

“Yes. But you will be able to read other people’s mind”

“So, what if I end up liking Renee as well?”

“Wait? You like Renee, our classmate?”

“I’m not crazy!”

“Calm down,” Iris laughed.

“Anyways, if you like Renee later on, you should need to confess and get rejected later on”

“Hey!!” Luscius shouted, frustrated.

“Kids!” Mrs Red called, in a warning tone.

“Blood! We aren’t kid’s mum!” They both shouted.

“Oh well, here we go,” Mrs Red shook her head.

Anna and Trevor walked into John’s cottage slowly. It was quite beautiful and nice; it was looking rich too.

After searching and calling his name for several minutes, they concluded he wasn't home.

"Where are you, John?" Anna said, worriedly.

"Let's just go. He must have gone to see his other magic buddies downtown"

"Wait" Anna said.

"What again?" I'm getting tired, you know" Trevor complained.

"Please, just wait."

"Wait?" What are you trying to do?"

"I'm going to check where he is and what happened before his disappearance"

"How?"

"What else?" With Magic?"

"We got another one" Someone suddenly said, and a lady holding the trigger of a gun came out from a hidden dark corner.

"So, where are we going?" Rose asked. Melissa linked her right arm with hers. She's in the middle of Rose and Lola and her arms are busily linked with both Lena and Doris arms.

"Let's just have fun first before going home," Melissa winked.

"Where exactly is this fun place?" Rose asked.

"Tada!! We're here!" Melissa exclaimed.

They all stopped walking and looked up to see an amusement park with an artificial horse ride, car ride, merry go round, etc.

They also sold cotton candies, ice creams, popcorn, lollipops, and beverages.

"Whoa. Never thought this place existed. Let's go" Michael said and jumped.

Rose sighed as she watched Michael go in. Melissa looked at her and smiled.

"What are you waiting for?" We had better hurry before all the seats get taken"

"Wait" Rose suddenly said, which made them not move an inch.

Melissa looked at her again.

"Why?"

Why are you doing this? You know. I really didn't treat you well today" Rose said softly, Melissa smiled.

“It's okay. I simply want to be your friend. You know we are seatmates, it’s better we aren’t harsh with the other” Rose's face formed a smile.

“Okay then… Let’s go”

“Found you” They all heard someone say. Before they could turn back to check, someone had already pulled Melissa's collar from behind

She flapped her lashes up to see Zeke smiling mischievously at her, at the corner end of his lips.

“Zeke?” Lola called in surprise.

“What’s he doing here?” Rose asked.

“What do you want?” Melissa asked.

Zeke slowly took his hand off her collar and pocketed his hands.

“I’ve been looking for you, you know

“Aww” Rose and Lola giggled.

“Hey, you both should stop,” Melissa shook her head. She deeply exhaled and faced him.

“So, why were you looking for me?” She asked.

She saw a little teddy bear that Jake had taken out. "Is this yours? He asked. “Huh?

How did you even get this? Melissa asked directly. Zeke answered, "I spotted it. On the floor."

"Please, return it. I value it’s a great deal. It's sentimental. It was a gift from my older sister for my birthday.

"I tie it around my backpack pack every time, I suppose it became unfastened and fell. She gave him an explanation and extended her hand to grab it, but he withdrew it.

"Wait a second, not so fast, no, no, no!" Zeke grinned

“What is it once this time?” Melissa asked.

"I'm going to return this to you, but there's a catch," he continued.

"What's that?" She asked.

"Take me out for dinner," he said.

"What!" She exclaimed.

"Is this love now?" Michael giggled.

"Aish! Keep shut, you" Melissa warned and then faced Jake.

"Okay then. A dinner, right?" Melissa asked and stretched her hand forth.

“Sure” Zeke said and placed it right on her hand. He turned to leave when Lena intelligent question shook him.

“How did you know it was hers?”

Zeke turned around.

“What?” He muttered, facing her.

Melissa was looking at him when Zeke turned to face her.

"What?” What? Again, what is it?”

“Why do you keep looking at me?” “What do you want from me?” She spoke quickly and requested.

"What's that?" She asked.

"Take me out for dinner," he said.

"What!" She exclaimed.

"Is this love now?" Michael giggled.

"Aish! Keep shut, you" Lissa warned and then faced Jake.

"Okay then. A dinner, right?" Lissa asked and stretched her hand forth.

"Sure" Jake said and placed it right on her hand. He turned to leave when Lena's intelligent question shook him.

"How did you know it was hers?"

Jake turned around.

"What?" He muttered, facing her.

"What's happening there?"

Red Mansion

The Red family were eating their lunch when Iris used her powers in bringing the jam close to her side on the table. Luscius was about to use it then.

"Hey" Luscius half yelled.

"Iris?" Mr Red called.

"Dad?" Iris answered cutely.

"What did I tell you about, using your powers?" Mr Red took down his cutlery.

"I always caution her. She's just too bloody stubborn" Mrs Red shook her head as she drank water.

"I'm sorry dad. I'm going to behave humanely just like Luscius I promise" Iris said.

Mr Red sighed and patted her hair.

"That's my girl." He said.

“What’s it now?” Melissa asked, folding her arms.

“Why did you speak for me then?”

“Why?” “Aren’t you glad that I did so?” you want them to suspect?”

“What?” Suspect?” Zeke scoffed.

“What do you know?” He asked, slowly coming closer to her.

“I know about you, Zeke”

“Huh?”

"You're a vampire. Luscius too."

"Did someone just call my name?" Luscius scratched his ear.

"You'd better eat and stop spewing trash" Iris eyed him.

"What was that?" My powers at work?" He thought and shook his head waving it aside.

"But?" But…

"Should I keep the names going?" Melissa asked.

“But I… made you-

“Forget?” She scoffed.

Zeke widened his eyes and stared at her face intensely.

Chapter 6: Differences

“You… Who the hell are you!”

"I'm Melissa. Who else would I be?"

"Oh, so that's how it's going to be huh?” Then let me rephrase that. *What* are you?"

"Wouldn't you like to know?"

"Yes, I very much will."

"Why the bloody hell should I answer your stupid question?” Who or what I am is none of your damn business, leech."

"You called me leech."

"I did, didn't I? So?"

"At least now I know you aren't human."

"Huh?"

"Only other supernatural's call know to call vampires 'leech'. That tone of contempt, a human would be scared or fascinated. You're not." Melissa felt like smacking her forehead.

"Aren't you just the world's greatest detective, Sherlock?"

Melissa took a deep breath and directed her lips toward his ear.

"Now, tell me what you think I am."

As her face moved back to his, Zeke laughed.

"Do you think I'm a vamp?"

Vampire my ass! He chuckled

"What?"

"You aren't a vampire, sweet blood"

“Stop calling me that”

“Vampires don't taste their fellow vampire blood or find it sweet. We know one when we see one. You aren’t a hybrid either. Besides, as I said, your contempt. Vampires don't just go around hating other vampires.” Zeke said.

"There are plenty of humans who hate other humans. Who knows, I might have had a traumatic experience with my kind in the past. How would you know?" Zeke just smiled and shook his head.

“Then, what am I? A sorceress? Just like Anna?”

“Seriously?” “Do you even know about her?” How much do you know?”

“A lot. and you haven't answered the question, Sherlock. Zeke, can you find out what I am, or can you not?” Zeke rubbed his forehead.

“What powers do you have?” He asked.

"It amuses me to no end that you think you can just ask and you will receive from me.

“Why should I tell you?"

"This is a guessing game, is it not? I’m entitled to being given some hints you know."

“I suppose you aren’t incorrect. Hmm, let's see... I can see what people truly are. Like if you’re a vampire, hybrid, magician, and all stuff like that. Also, their powers don’t work on me-

Zeke scoffed. "Of course. That's because you’re a not human yourself. I know all this. Blood, a child will know all this. How about you tell me something I don't know."

"Alright, alright. Hmm how about...ah, yes. I can charm people. “How about now?"

Zeke cocked his head. "An enchantress, a succubus, siren?" Come on, there are dozens with the power to charm. Can't you be more specific?"

“What’s it now?” Melissa frowned. Anymore and he will find out. Well, she supposed she was growing weary of this. She sighed

"I can talk to fish, and swim. Very fast."

He snapped his fingers. "A bloody mermaid. Wow. Didn't know there were any of you left. Aren't you a little too far from home?"

"You don't say."

Zeke cupped his chin with his hand.

“This means you remembered everything. Including the- Zeke paused and cleared his throat.

“The kiss?” Melissa asked.

Zeke looked at her and widened his eyes. He looked down and took his eyes back to her.

"Why are you even nonchalant?" You don't seem fazed or shocked?" Zeke asked.

"Why would I?" The kiss doesn't mean anything so-

Zeke laughed.

"It was your first kiss, dummy"

"So? First kisses are nothing. It's the last kiss that matters most, ``she said.

“Whatever. Just continue what we were saying” “Uhm… Also, I heal fast”

“What?”

"I can do magic, not charm, real magic. It's small but, it's there."

"Mermaids can't do that."

"No shit Sherlock."

"Are you a hybrid then?"

“Yeah”

"Which side?" Of mermaid and what?"

"Mother was mermaid. Father, don't know."

"Are you a demigoddess?" He asked.

"Is that what I am?" She asked, back.

"I don't know. Just asking" He replied. Melissa shook her head.

"Now, I know why you always get a F, despite being a powerful vampire"

"Hey, how do you know… I got a F?"

Melissa pointed at her head.

"I told you. I have powers I can't apprehend... What I just need you to help me do is to find out who I am"

"Alright... but as for now, don't tell anyone of your powers"

"Huh? Got that"

"But can you read minds?"

"Minds?" No... I can't. I just know things about people and even the supernatural. I know what they are."

"Melissa?" "Will you two keep talking?" We've been waiting and it's almost 5pm already" They heard Lena's voice.

They turned around and saw her with a slight frown on her face. Her hands were crossed together, as she stared at them.

"I'm sorry for keeping y'all waiting" she said. Melissa looked at Zeke

"Later" She whispered and left with Rose

"Huh? Where's Michael?" Melissa looked around, after only seeing Lola and Rose

"He left. He's tired of waiting so he decided to go home" Rose said.

“Hmm. Hope I ain’t wasting your time “Let’s go have fun!!” Rose screamed joyously and ran to the spinning wheel.

Melissa smiled and ran to them.

The three girls enjoyed themselves, they bought snacks, and licked ice cream. They rode a lot of fun machinery and took lots of cute and funny pictures in the photo booth.

“Wow, It's so cute. Look at Lola's face” Rose smiled as they all walked out, looking at the pictures on Lissa’s hand.

“Here” Melissa handed Rose one of the pictures.

Rose smiled and collected it.

“Lola, here” Melissa handed her one which she took.

“I’m going to take two,” Melissa smiled, and the girls laughed. “Man! That was fun” Rose giggled.

“I swear,” Lola agreed, as they walked out of sight.

Dora’s Home

Rose inhaled deeply and walked in. She was really scared. She held her bag straps at both sides as she walked in nervously.

“Rose? You are late” It was her father’s hoarse voice.

Rose sighed and turned to face him. He was reading a newspaper with small glasses on his fat face.

“Dad, I-

“Michael told me you were at a study group class. That’s good” Mr Dora smiled.

“Huh?” Rose breathed heavily.

“Yes, I…I was quite busy studying. Our mid-term test is in a few weeks. I know how angry you are going to get if I flop this exam-

You’re already flopping it” Her father’s harsh voice said. He took down the newspaper and looked at her.

“Dad, I don’t understand” Rose forced a chuckle.

"Upon the money I spend and the tutorial you attend, you still can't be at the top" he said.

"Dad, I'm trying though. I'm the sec- "I don't want you to be the second! What happened to the first?" Is that person a supernatural being, two headed or what?! If you don't take the top position this time around, I'm going to kill you"

"Just like the way you hit me as usual?" Rose scoffed.

"What did you say?"

"Why don't you kill me now! Just like the way you killed Mum!!" She screamed, crazily.

"Have you gone mad!" He thundered and rose to his feet.

"You could have just killed me earlier the moment you saw my face for the first time after mum gave birth to me! "Why make my life a living hell!"

"You! Where did you leave your brains? At school!" He yelled and threw the hard spoon which was on the table.

It hit her eye hard, and she quickly closed it. She whimpered in pain slowly.

"Dad, please" Michael quickly came to her in order to shield her from the mug his father wanted to throw at her.

“Take her away!” He snapped.

“Or it's her corpse they will be taking away” He added.

Michael breathed and held her hand. He took her away and when they went upstairs to her room door, she quickly took her arm away from his hand.

“Rose…I-

“I hate him”

“Rose, your eyes… It’s swollen and it’s getting dark, let me help-"

"I hate you too," She whispered.

"What?"

"Dad treats you differently. I'm just the black sheep for being second and you are the nice son for being just... nothing" she said, slowly, raising her eyes to him.

"Rose, you know I don't understand why either"

"We both understand!!"

"Rose"

"I'm jealous," She whispered.

Michael sighed heavily and looked down.

"I wish you would just die"

Michael quickly looked at her.

"Rose. Why are you talking like this?"

"Maybe if you died, Dad might finally love me, what do you think?"

"You should rest and add some ointment to your eyes before it finally closes and darkens" Michael said and left.

Rose opened the door and went to her huge bed. She laid down on it and kept her face down, crying hard.

“Dad, I’m home!” She heard her elder sister’s voice say from downstairs.

Rose wiped her tears and sat down.

“Another one I’m jealous of,” She muttered.

“How was work, Jessica?” She heard her father ask.

“Uurgh! Stressful Daddy. And it's because of a new wrench at work” She had replied.

Rose inhaled deeply and opened her cupboard. She took out the ointment which was in a tube.

“It is almost finished. Guess I’ll have to get another” She whispered before applying it on her eyes.

Lake’ Home

The two sisters ate the mashed yam and egg sauce from their different bowls while seated on the sofa. They were watching a soap opera.

“Girls?” Lorna called.

They didn’t reply though. Their eyes were on the TV, and they weren’t concentrating.

"Girls?!" Lorna called again, raising her voice. They looked at her.

"Yes, Noona?" They answered, simultaneously.

"How… was your school, Morgan's High?" She asked.

"Fine… just too fine" Lola smiled.

Lorna nodded and faced Melissa

"What about you, Melissa?" How was school?"

Melissa blinked her eyes. "Weird."

“Weird? “How weird?” Did you… did you see

“The school toilets are funny,” Melissa said.

“Eh?” Lorna blinked her eyes

“There was a clock in there”

“Huh? Oh, that wasn’t what I was talking about” Lorna said.

“So, what were you talking about?” Melissa asked.

"I mean, weird-weird. Powerful weird" Lorna shook her head.

"What's she talking about?" Doris asked.

Melissa shrugged her shoulders.

"Wished I knew"

Lorna sighed.

"You both should be careful and don't ask me why. Also, just in case you see something weird there. Let me know, got that?"

They both nodded.

“Melissa?” Lorna called.

“Noona?” Melissa answered.

“How are you now?” This morning, you

“I’m better. I guess I was just sick”

“Are you better now?”

“As you can see”

Lorna bit her lower lip, suspiciously.

“Melissa? Don’t hesitate to share anything with me, anything bothering you. There’s something I need to show you”

Melissa nodded and stood up.

“Sure”

“If she gets weak, I might think otherwise” Lorna thought.

“Let’s go!” She smiled and stood up.

Lorna opened the door.

“Go in,” she said.

“Huh? Noona. You changed the lights?” Whoa” Melissa smiled, looking at it from outside.

“Yes, now, let’s both go in. I wanna show you something” Lorna said, and Melissa nodded.

Chapter 7: Interference

"Melissa? You, okay?" Lorna asked, bringing her back to her senses.

Melissa blinked her eyes and looked at her. She chuckled awkwardly and sat down.

"Yeah, I'm great. But…but does it have to be there?" I mean Farrow Lane. Why not somewhere else.

"That's the best place, Lissa. Trust me. You're going to love it"

"I wish" Lissa whispered and rolled her eyes.

"As soon as you leave for school, A truck will come over to move our things to our new home so… you just have to go to 12, Furrow Lane, okay?"

"Sure… Sure" Melissa replied.

"Urrgh" Lola grunted.

"Girls? Come on" Lorna pouted.

"Noona… We know, we know" They replied, simultaneously.

Ocean's High

“Okay, Class. Hope you understand?” The teacher asked, closing her books.

“Yes, Sir!” They all replied, with the usual tone.

“Okay, good. See y’all in the next class and don’t forget your assignments”

“Yes, Sir!”

The teacher nodded and left the class and the instant he did, students left their seats and started making noises.

“Urgh!” Zeke groaned and raised his head up. He was sleeping during class.

“The noise in this class is unbearable, makes me wanna kill them! Urgh! This is exactly why I prefer when there’s no class going on”

He groaned again before placing his head down.

“Whoa. Anna. Guess who came to school today?” Nora winked.

“What are you saying?” Anna eyed her.

“Him… John” Nora gestured with her head.

“So?” Anna glanced at him.

“He wasn’t here yesterday, and you were absolutely worried,” Nora chuckled.

"Who said I was?" Anna scoffed.

Iris looked at John and then at the girls.

"By the way, Is John sick?" Iris asked.

"What's it?" Anna asked.

"He keeps staring at me and I can't tell or read his mind cause he's a fucking supernatural being" she said and looked away.

Anna turned to look at John at the back and really saw him looking at Iris.

“What’s wrong with him?” She thought.

Anna inhaled deeply and stood up. She walked to him and placed her palm on his forehead.

“What are you doing?” He smacked her hand away.

“Hey, what’s wrong with you?” Anna quickly asked.

“What are you saying?” He asked, glaring hard at her.

“You’re so hot. You look sick too”

“I’m okay. Don’t pry into my health life” he said and looked away.

Anna bit her lips and sat on his desk.

"Hey, what's with you and staring at Iris?" Do… you have feelings for her?" She asked.

John slowly looked at her with his cold eyes.

"So, what if I do?" He asked.

"Huh?" You do?"

"Get lost" He flatly said.

"Hey, John. "What's your qualms now?" Anna asked, with teary eyes.

John didn't reply.

"I was so worried about you, I even looked around for you and went to your cottage

"So? Trevor did so too, and he isn't blabbing about it"

"Hey! Do you even know we saw a dark hun-

"Damn!!" He shouted, stood up quickly and slammed his palm on his desk, loudly.

Everyone kept quiet and looked at him.

"You are… fucking annoying" He whispered and left the class.

Anna ran after him with tears in her eyes, while everyone watched.

“Oww!” John whimpered after feeling something hit his head. He quickly turned around to see Anna in tears.

He saw her shoe beside him.

“Hey! Did you throw that at me!” He screamed. “Oww!” He screamed again after she threw her other shoe at his forehead without thinking twice.

“Hey! What was that for!” He asked.

“You don’t care about me, do you?” Even if I’m on the edge of death, you won’t still save me, will you?” I guess I’m the only one feeling this way! I think, I like you”

John scoffed.

“Keep that to yourself! I don’t wanna hear it

“Then, why did you hug me! You’re a jerk! “Why did you hug me that night?”

“You hugged me first!” John said.

“Then, why didn’t you stop me or push me away?” Why did you return the damn hug!”

John looked at her briefly.

"You aren't my type, Anna. You know that you should get your act together! That hug isn't a big deal" he said and began walking away.

"Then, tell me what happened to you last night?" Was it the Grim Hunters?" "Did they take you?"

John stopped and turned back to her.

"Are you hoping it could have been them?" He asked, with a smirk on his face.

"John?"

He breathed hard and walked away, Anna watched him with tears in her eyes. She fell to her knees, crying out loud in the silent corridor.

John pushed the toilet's door open, he squeezed his face and sat down on the toilet seat.

The venom in his body was hitting him real hard, it was hurting him.

He kept panting, he sighed deeply and wiped the sweat off his face.

"Should I bring Iris to them, instead?" He thought.

> "Oh! She's Anna's friend. She might feel hurt. Luscius? … No, He's a hybrid. Trevor? Am I crazy?

"Why would I include my best friend?" Zeke? He's… quite better, Ow… This really hurts, ``he said, and quickly stood up.

"Dam" He sobbed.

"Why did you bring me here?" Melissa asked, looking at the empty classroom.

Zeke looked around and then turned to her, he had a smile on his face. Soon, Iris and Luscius came in. Trevor also entered, then, Anna and Nora.

"Hey, is this everybody? What of John?" Zeke looked around.

“He says he isn’t interested,” Trevor replied. Anna stole a glance at Trevor and quickly looked away.

“So, why did you call us here? You’d better hurry. I have books to read. Our midterm tests are coming up” Luscius said.

“Hey, Iris?” Zeke called.

“Huh, Brother?” Iris replied.

“Do you ever give your brother a reminder that he’s a hybrid?” Zeke asked.

Nora and Trevor laughed while Anna had her sad look on. Iris just shrugged her shoulders. “Hmm. Melissa, seat down” He gestured.

There was only a stool there and that was what she used to sit on.

"Now, everyone. Melissa is… a mermaid. A half mermaid to be exact."

"What?" They all exclaimed except Luscius and Anna.

"That's why her sweet blood wasn't ordinary. Whoa" Nora said.

"Hey. What are you doing?" Melissa asked Zeke. She tried to stand up, but Zeke quickly held her down.

"Keep calm, sweetie" He winked.

“What?” Melissa stuttered.

“Now, tell them your powers so we can all start getting on which supernatural being category you fall in”

“I’m going to ask again, what do you think you are doing, Zeke?”

“Why?” You asked me to help” He smirked.

“By telling everyone?” She muttered.

“I’m out,” Anna said, abruptly and left.

"Hey, what's the witch's problem now?" Zeke asked.

Iris looked at the door and sighed.

"I don't know" She shook her head.

"Now, what are your powers? Just tell us. Your secrets are safe with us" Nora winked.

"My secrets are safe with y'all because we are supernatural" Melissa rolled her eyes.

Nora folded her lips and took a few steps backwards.

“Anyways, since she doesn’t wanna talk. I’m going to do it, on her behalf” Zeke said.

Luscius watched him and crossed his arms.

“No power takes an effect on her. She also feels less pain and her wounds stitches up immediately.

She knows who and what someone is after looking at the person, and she can do magic.

All not your usual mermaid powers.. Is that all?” Zeke asked.

“Oh… Oh… She has this sweet blood” He added, chuckling.

Melissa shook her head.

“Also, Hmm, I know where someone is at that moment and what the person is doing, ``she said.

“Like?” Luscius asked, now getting curious.

“Wait. “Can you check on the principal?” “Where’s she?” What’s she doing now?” Iris asked, quickly.

They all looked at her. Melissa sighed and looked at the space. She blinked and started talking.

“Mrs Morgan. She’s 42. Principal Of Ocean’s High. Right now, she’s in her office, and she is… she… is…is

"Hey, Talk. "What's she doing?" Iris asked, curiously, with bulging eyes.

Melissa curved her brows and inhaled deeply.

"Right now, she is crying"

"What?" They all asked.

"No, why?" Nora asked.

"Don't know since the reason doesn't come out," Melissa replied.

"Oh, I see," Zeke smiled.

"Melissa?" They all heard a small voice.

They all turned to the door only to see Lola looking at them.

"Melissa. Why… are you here? What…what are you saying?" Lola quavered.

Melissa quickly stood up.

"I can explain.

"Don't come close!!" Lola yelled and clenched her fist with her eyes getting wet already.

"Why tell them?"

Chapter 8: Mischief

“Lola!” Melissa screamed and ran out of the room, outside.

She hurried past Iris who was walking in the opposite direction.

Melissa was coming down when Iris paused and turned to look.

“What? Melissa? Why is she in this place? Iris muttered something.

“Stop!” Melissa yelled while laboriously panting. When Lola stopped and seemed to be held up, two large bullies from Ocean's High caught her attention.

“Do you both have a death wish?” Melissa glared at them.

The two bullies exchanged glances and laughed.

“Who’s this little morsel?” One said.

“I guess she is the one who has a death wish” The other said, and they both laughed again.

Melissa smirked.

“You both are messing with the wrong being,” she said. The bully scoffed.

“Why?” You’re supernatural?” He scoffed.

“Melissa shrugged her shoulders.

They hurried to her in order to hit her while she remained strong and stiff.

Few Minutes Later

“Kneel!” The bully orders.

Lola looked at Melissa as she knelt next to her and snorted.

Lola yelled, "Fool.

“Why are you trying to save me?” Even fighting is impossible. You should have at least pleaded, she said.

Melissa sighed and looked at her hands, it was reddish and sore. They had hit her and pushed her around. She had a cut on her thigh, but it quickly healed.

“What a waste of supernatural powers. I don’t even have supernatural strength” Melissa thought.

“You!” The bully pointed.

“Yes?” Melissa answered quickly.

“What’s that on your neck?” The bully asked and Lola quickly looked.

“Oh no. Not that” Lola shook her head.

Melissa blinked her eyes and touched the pendent.

“My mother gave me

The bully hit her face.

“I never asked you who gave you. I said, `

“What's that?”

Melissa held her tears from pouring out.

“It's a pendant,” She replied.

“A pendant?” Nice, take it off” The bully said, and the other chuckled.

“No, I can't,” Melissa said, slowly.

“What?” The bully hit her head and took her up from the harsh ground where she knelt on.

“Say it again? You say what?” The bully asked, holding her arm tight like he wanted to rip it off.

Melissa's tears fell.

"No, I won't give it to you. Anything but this" she said, with a shaky voice.

"Guess what I'll do when you don't hand the pendant to me?" The bully smiled evilly.

Melissa looked deeply at him.

"Denario Fungus. 19, A 6th grader at Ocean's High, only child of his poor parents.

Why?" Do you live like that?" Aren't your parents trying hard?"

"Huh?" The bully's eyes twitched.

"How do you know…about me? How!"

He asked, shouting.

Lola just watched.

"Who's she?" The other yelled coming closer. Melissa quickly looked at him.

"Gumy Kruger. 18 years old. A truant. Fifth son of heiress Mileena…

"Shut up!" Denario smacked her mouth causing Melissa's face to turn. She sighed and took her face at him.

"How do you know these things and how much more do you know?" Gumy asked.

"I know more than you can ever imagine," Melissa said.

"She talks too much. She won't give us the pendant either" Denario said.

Gumy looked at Denario hand clenching onto Melissa's small arm, he smiled and walked close to Denario.

"Tom?" Gumy whispered.

"Huh?" Denario answered.

“Just break an arm,” Martin said.

“What?” Denario asked.

“Break her arm, then let’s deal with this little girl’s honey pot” Gumy looked at Lola who sacredly shifted back.

Denario smiled and looked at Melissa who was quite scared trying to act strong.

“Ah” Melissa's voice shook as her arm started getting twisted by Denario. “Does it hurt?” I like” Denario winked, dangerous as he twisted it the more.

"Ah!" Melissa screamed endlessly as she watched her arm get twisted in the other direction. She also heard her bones breaking and cracking.

Iris walked into the sitting room and saw Luscius reading a novel, while sitting on the couch with his legs folded on the table. On the table was a glass of milk.

Iris walked to him and carried the glass of milk to her mouth. Luscius looked at her angrily as she drank the milk finish.

"Why didn't you eat the bottle too?" Like, I bought it for you" Luscius snarled.

"Whatever" Iris rolled her eyes

She belched satisfiedly and Luscius let out a sound of disgust.

“Yuck! Behave yourself” he said. “Don’t behave like you don’t do that too, Smart pants. Anyways, I saw Melissa around here” Iris said.

“Yeah. She lives close by, few blocks away” Luscius said.

“What?” Few blocks away?” No, I saw her running down the street, away from the blocks”

“What?” Luscius quickly stood up.

“You sure?”

"Yeah. Seems she forgot something, or Iris paused after Luscius swiftly ran away.

"Uh?" "Where did he go?" Oh well" She shrugged her shoulders and left for her room.

Luscius moved his nose, as he tried smelling where Melissa was.

"Why isn't this working?" Disadvantages of a hybrid" He muttered.

He slowly took off his glasses and at once, used his powers in getting an unremarkable view of where Melissa was.

He saw Melissa being bullied and he gasped loudly.

“Shit, He half yelled and quickly ran off.

"Say your prayers." Said the bastard Denario, raising his fist.

Then, from nowhere, Luscius enters the scene with a mean right hook thrown at Denario, sending him flying crashing to the ground, cracking it. "Aaah!"

Gumy sees this and moves to intercept when Melissa seeing her chance worked her magic.

Her mere-abilities rather, as she didn't quite trust her magic that much.

She spun the moisture in the air till she got a drop of water the size of a bullet and shot it at Gumy's stupid face, piercing his eye.

"Aaah!" He screamed. "My eye!" Zeke came to meet him "Aww, something wrong with it? Here, let me take a look at it."

He punched him right there, in the bleeding socket with enough force to knock him out.

Then he looked at the girls. "You girls okay?"

"Yeah," they said. "Thanks," Lola said to him. The she turned to Melissa. "You and I, we gotta talk. But later.

I need to hit the sheets." She left. Then Luscious and Melissa stared at each other for a while.

Their eyes burning at each other's in gratitude, concern, relief and budding. Love?

"Lucy?"

"Yeah?" "Take me home."

"Will do."

Chapter 9: Romance

They entered Melissa's room kissing, Luscius then leans back "I'm going to drink you now," he says , grabbing a fistful of her hair and tilting her head to the side.

The smooth, skin of her neck was just begging to be licked and sucked.

After a moment, he do just that. His saliva marks the sensitive skin there, and Lissa's breath hitches sharply. Then he bit down.

"Aahh" Lissa moaned. Her blood enters his mouth, eliciting feelings and sensations they have never felt before, causing moans to reverberate through their body.

"Fuck," he breathes huskily, his hips jerking upwards. His own moan rumbles through his chest.

She gyrate my hips against his. Each thrust causes his cock to hit her sweet spot, even with the two layers of clothing separating them.

They fall to the bed, they undress each other. Zeke enters her with a soft grunt, making Lissa's breath to catch as he begins to move.

Her body under his as he thrust into her, those perfect tits bouncing in his face.

Then, his demeanor changes, and he pounds into her brutally and savagely.

She goes from crying his name to shouting it. She clenched around him, heat rushing to her core.

"Oh, Mother of Pearl." She squeezed her eyes shut.

This was what she wanted, she knew exactly what she was getting myself into with Zeke, she loved it.

His teeth were on her neck, nibbling softly as he took gentle sips from her.

"Tell me what you want, Lissa."

“You” she threw her head back. “Please don’t stop…”

“Say it again,” he murmured. “I love the way you say my name.”

She moaned, toes curling. “You, Zeke. I want you.”

"That's a good girl." His fingers quickened, and soon her legs were trembling as wave after wave of ecstasy rolled through her.

“He leaned into her ear and whispered”

"You’re mine now, Lissa. For all eternity."

END OF BOOK

www.ingramcontent.com/pod-product-compliance
Lightning Source LLC
LaVergne TN
LVHW090925150826
845672LV00006B/1399

* 9 7 9 8 8 4 7 4 0 6 1 4 7 *